The Dragons of Kilve

On a wild, rocky shore not far from here,
five dragon eggs are cracking.
The mischief, fun and adventure are about to begin...

Twelve delightful short stories for younger readers.

*'A beautiful book, full of wisdom and very funny.
Children will love it.'* Mrs Mad's Book-a-Rama

*'A charming book for children... Beth Webb uses her
mischievous and lively little dragons to explore some
very big issues indeed.'* Just Women Magazine

Beth Webb lives in Somerset.
Kilve is a real place, and her dragons are real too
– *if you want them to be!*

Her other children's titles include the Fleabag series
and Junkyard Dragon. She has also written the Star
Dancer quartet for teenagers.

www.bethwebb.co.uk
www.stardancerbooks.com

For Gabriel and Gabrielle
who first told me about the dragons

Acknowledgments

My thanks to Gabriel and Maddy
for helping to think up the stories.
Also to John and Tom.

Why not?

The Dragons of Kilve

Beth Webb

With illustrations by

Jenny Press

Best wishes
Beth Webb

MHM
March Hamilton Media

Contents

The Dawn of Time

*L*ong ago, when the world was young and the moon still sang at night, many strange and wonderful creatures roamed the earth.

These were the stuff of dreams and legends – and most were best avoided.

Beneath the deepest seas, the great serpent Leviathan peered hungrily through the endless dark with baleful eyes. She was so long she could twist her luminous tail three *times around the world.*

She had a cousin, the fiery Behemoth who lurked in the molten depths of the boiling earth, guarding deadly secrets.

Lurking under a wet stone, or maybe wedged in a crack, the slug-like Nidhogg oozed slime and plotted havoc.

More kindly were the unicorns that tossed their milky manes as they cantered across sunlit fields. Freedom and wind were the blood of their veins.

Above them all rose flights of dragons, some gold, some red, others purple and pink. And in a rocky bay not so far from where we sit, lived the mischievous blue-green dragons of Kilve.

Each of these beasts had a friendly Master or a Mistress, to help them when the world became too difficult or strange.

The Dragon Master was every bit as exciting as his creatures. He was as old as time, with wild hair and a hooked nose. His piercing eyes took the colour of the sea, whatever the weather. Draped in his deep blue cloak of stars, the Dragon Master wandered ceaselessly about the earth, watching and caring for his winged friends.

And these are some of his tales…

Horrible Horace

The dragons of Kilve had blue-green bodies and silver wings. Their eyes gleamed like huge rubies and their claws were curved and bright.

When the morning skies were brim-full of sunshine, the dragons soared between the clouds and dived the seas for fish. In the evenings they stretched out on the cool stony shore beside the Dragon Master, and together they sang and told stories, boasted of feats of flight, laughed at jokes and scratched each other's scales. Sometimes, they walked along the cliff tops as the sun slipped silently into the sea.

In the chilly darkness, the weary dragons curled up under the Dragon Master's cloak of stars, and slept.

With gentle dreams, he took the dragons' sorrows away so each morning started fresh.

One sparkling dawn was particularly exciting, for at the back of a cave, a long-forgotten dragon egg was beginning to crack. By lunchtime, a tiny, turquoise hatchling had crawled out from the leathery shell, shaken his transparent wings and yawned.

The older dragons were delighted and they called him Horace. It was many years since they'd had a new baby so whatever Horace wanted, he got.

Flamethrower built him a beautiful rocky nest lined with seaweed. But then he had to move it, for Horace didn't like the cave it was in.

Igneous spent all day catching the fattest fish because Horace was always hungry. But he would eat only cod, so the older dragons were left with the mackerel, which was rather indigestible.

Others brought treasures from their own hoards for Horace to play with. Ember found a mermaid's hair ribbon and hung a crystal on it to catch the light. Fireworks performed coloured smoke displays and deaf old Fizzle smuggled him chocolate biscuits when Ember wasn't looking.

Everyone adored Horace – but he was getting fatter and greedier.

One day he was lying on his back, sunning his

tummy, when suddenly he pointed a long silver claw towards the sky.

'*Want*!' he demanded. '*Gimme*!'

'What, dear?' asked Ember.

'Ball!'

'I can't see a ball, dear.'

'*That* ball. *Gimme*!'

Ember looked up to where Horace was pointing. 'That's not a ball, dear, that's the sun,' she said kindly.

'*Want*!' he screamed.

Hearing the rumpus, the other dragons swooped down from the sky, crawled out of the sea and gathered around.

'What's up?' demanded Igneous.

'Has a crab pinched his tail?' Furnace asked.

'Maybe the Nidhogg's nibbled his nose?' Flamethrower growled, looking around nervously.

When Pumice told them what was going on, they laughed, which made Horace even crosser, and he howled for the rest of that day.

When the Dragon Master came in the evening, everyone was too tired and upset to talk, so he pulled his cloak of stars over them all and hoped they would get some sleep.

Day after day, things got worse. Horace grew thin and pale and his scales dropped like turquoise leaves. He wanted the golden ball so much!

At last, the dragons could stand no more. They could not bear to see their only baby so ill – and they were quite worn out with worry. They no longer walked with the Dragon Master at sunset. They forgot to hug and laugh together. Everyone was very unhappy. Something had to be done.

'There's nothing for it,' Flamethrower sighed. 'Tomorrow, we'll have to fetch the sun down for Horace. He'll soon learn it's too hot to play with.'

Next morning, leaving Pumice the old wingless dragon to look after baby Horace, Flamethrower led the dragons spiralling into the sky, and between them they carried a huge bag.

Up and up they flew, but as they climbed, the sun became so big, bright and hot, they couldn't breathe and their wings ached. They dropped the bag and one by one they fell spinning and twisting back down to the sea. Wet and exhausted, they crawled into their caves.

They didn't even notice the Dragon Master sadly spreading his dark cloak and lighting the stars.

Next day, the dragons decided that instead of

flying *up* to get the sun, they'd fly west in the evening and catch it as it sank *down* into the sea.

So they flew to the Midnight Forest and cut a tall pine tree. They chewed off the branches until it was just a long pole with a fork at the top. Then they tied a strong seaweed net to the prongs.

They were going fishing for the sun!

As evening approached they set off towards the sunset. Now dragons can fly extremely far and fast, but however hard they flew, the sun was always just ahead. Before long it turned gold and slipped silently into the sea.

Exhausted, the dragons found a rocky island and slept.

At breakfast next morning, everyone was tired and miserable. Then Flamethrower had an idea. 'Let's set off really early and we're bound to get to the west before the sun does.'

Cheered by such a brilliant plan, the dragons took off. The sun rose hot and burned their tails, then it arched higher and scorched their backs. At last it slid ahead of them, glowed orange on their noses and sank into the sea once more.

On and on the dragons flew into the dark, beating the air with their aching wings and looking for somewhere to land.

Just before dawn when the air was filled with silvery light, Flamethrower pointed a claw. Look!' he roared. 'There are hills ahead – and – it's *Kilve*!'

'Don't be silly!' scoffed the others. 'We've flown for two days. We must be thousands of miles away!'

'Then we've gone in a circle!' Flamethrower groaned, gliding a steep spiral down to the rocky beach below.

One by one all the other dragons landed next to him. And there they stayed in exhausted heaps until the Dragon Master found them.

'I've been so worried about you,' he said sadly as he rubbed ointment into their sunburn. 'Pumice has told me what's been going on. Why didn't you let me help?'

The dragons hung their heads. Ember eased a weary wing back into shape. 'Do *you* know how to catch the sun?' she asked.

'I can do all sorts of things,' the Dragon Master chuckled. 'Bring me a big bucket of water and your bad baby dragon.'

So they did.

The Dragon Master had a little talk with Horace about not whining for things he couldn't have, and how he'd put the big dragons to a lot of trouble.

Then Horace said, 'Sorry' to everyone and there

were lots of 'I still love you' hugs.

Then the Dragon Master put the bucket in front of Horace. 'Now look,' he said.

And shimmering on the water's surface shone... *The sun*!

'Ball!' squeaked the baby dragon, grabbing for it with his claws. Then he started to cry loudly. 'Ball broken!' he wailed.

'Just wait,' said the Dragon Master.

The water stilled and Horace clapped his wings with delight. 'Ball back!' he giggled.

Now,' said the Dragon Master firmly, 'you can play that game as long as the sun is high. But when the bucket goes dark, you'll know it's time to come and look for me.'

'But what happens if we need you when the sun is still in the bucket?' asked Ember, who liked everything done properly.

The Dragon Master laughed and scratched Ember behind her ear. He pointed to the glittering light in the bucket. 'I'm here now, aren't I? I'm never far away, especially if you really need me.'

Fire Games

Not everyone was thrilled at Horace's arrival.
Two lazy young dragons called Igneous and
Furnace were very fed up with fetching and carrying
for a whinging baby – so they ran away to the
Midnight Forest. There they played hide-and-seek
behind the great oaks and sunbathed in the clearings.
The forest was cool, leafy and dark, very different
from Kilve's wide skies and sea.

Igneous and Furnace were having the time of their
lives on their own but after a while they grew bored
and their games became silly – then dangerous!

It was Igneous who began it. He'd been lying on
his back scratching his tummy when he sat up and

pointed a claw, 'See that dead tree that looks like Pumice's tail?'

Furnace opened one eye. 'So?'

Rolling over, Igneous flapped his wings and blew. Fire engulfed the tree. Orange flames roared and the wood crumbled into smoky ash. Igneous jumped around, snorting with glee.

Furnace wasn't impressed. 'Pah! Easy! That was a *dead* tree. I bet you can't burn a *green* one…'

'Bet I can,' Igneous grinned. Then *wooomph*! A lovely oak went up in flames.

'That's nothing!' Furnace roared, turning a tall pine into a column of fire.

Soon the two dragons were thudding along the riverbank, looking for the greenest, dampest places and bigger and bigger targets for their fire games. By sunset, whole stretches of the Midnight Forest lay ruined and the night was noisy with terrified birds and animals.

Far to the north on the rocky shores of Kilve, the Dragon Master smelled the fire and he set off for the forest, chewing his beard with worry.

As he drew close, the Dragon Master heard the cries of the homeless creatures. He wiped away a tear. He had to hurry. Things were bad!

In the early morning, the Dragon Master found

Igneous and Furnace boiling a pond dry and stamping on the fleeing animals.

'What are you bad dragons up to?' he roared.

'Having fun!' they yelled back.

Splat! Furnace swatted a golden-eyed toad. 'Gottcha!'

'Stop!' the Dragon Master yelled.

'Why should we?' Igneous sneered.

'Because you're hurting things that are smaller than you.'

'So what?' Furnace chuckled. 'Serves 'em right for being squelchy.' And he popped a caddis-fly larva between his claws.

'That was going to be a beautiful creature one day...' The Dragon Master began.

'Too late!' Furnace chuckled as he turned to Igneous. 'It's not very friendly around here. Shall we find somewhere quieter to play?'

'Right behind you,' Igneous replied, and stomped after his friend through the blacked trees, his green-blue tail swishing wildly.

The Dragon Master sat with his head in his hands. 'This is terrible, how can I stop them?' he asked aloud.

'Ahem,' a gruff voice coughed politely.

Looking up, the Dragon Master saw a magnificent lion with a shaggy brown mane. 'If I may be so bold,' he began, 'I will talk to them. I am the king of the beasts, they must obey me!'

The Dragon Master wasn't at all sure, but he said, 'Very well, but please be careful.'

The lion shook his mane and roared, then he leaped after the bad dragons who were very pleased to see him.

They had him for lunch.

As Igneous and Furnace were picking fur from their fangs, the Dragon Master arrived. He was so cross his face turned scarlet, white, then purple and steam blew out of his ears.

'What's the problem?' Furnace asked innocently. 'He was *almost* our size and we are dragons, we *have* to eat meat.'

The Dragon Master stormed away, sat quietly on a not-too burned log and tried to listen to the West Wind to see what it suggested. Just as he settled down, four yellow-stripy snakes wriggled over to him. 'My name's SSStanley. Thisss isss SSSidney, SSSam and SSSarah,' he said. 'We and the owlsss have an exsssellent plan to ssstop the dragonsss.'

'No, you mustn't. It's too dangerous,' the Dragon Master protested.

'Trusssst usssss,' Sarah insisted. 'Once the dragonsss are asssssleep, we will make our move.'

When Igneous and Furnace settled down for an after-lion snooze, the snakes tied themselves into scaly knots around the dragons' feet. Then, without a stir of wind, the owls flew in and gripped the dragons' wings with their sharp claws. This was important, because, as you know, if a dragon cannot flap its wings, it cannot take a *really* big breath, and without doing that, it cannot blow fire.

The two dragons woke up screaming, 'Help! Leggo!' But the more they wriggled, the tighter the brave creatures hung on.

At last Igneous and Furnace gave in. 'We'll do anything you say,' they moaned. 'Only let go, *please.*'

But the owls dug their claws in harder and the snakes tightened their coils one more turn. Now lisssten,' hissed Sam. 'We will hang onto you forever if you don't ssstop your wicked fire gamesss.'

'We promise! We promise!' the dragons howled. 'Only leggo! *Stoppit!*'

'And you-hoo will go-o away from the Midnight Forest and not come back?' demanded the owls.

'Yes! *Anything!*' sobbed Furnace.

'Very well,' and with a flutter of feathers and a rustling of scales, the snakes and the owls freed their captives.

But, sad to say, as soon as they let go, the terrible

dragons burst out laughing. They laughed until they cried, sending boiling streams of tears down their red-hot noses. They snorted, spluttered and giggled, rolling in the charcoal dust and kicking their legs in the air.

'Ho, ho! What a joke!' squealed Furnace.

'This really is too funny!' howled Igneous. They thrashed about with their long tails until the ground shook.

'Stop it and behave!' the Dragon Master shouted. '*What* is so funny?'

'It's... It's... it's juuuust... Oh hoo hoooo! My tummy aches!' Furnace was almost choking.

Igneous rolled over. 'It's just... we don't give... a... oh ho, oh no!' and they started laughing again.

At last, Furnace spluttered, 'It-hic-it's just we don't give a-hic-fig for promises. We kept our claws crossed so we don't have to do what we said!' Then to prove the point, the bad dragon ate the brave old snake and blew a burning yellow plume of fire into the sky.

'How *dare* you!' the Dragon Master roared. He itched to do something really nasty back. But he had to think of something better. Something that would make them feel sorry for what they were doing.

Meanwhile Igneous and Furnace stamped away, blasting like volcanoes. By nightfall the sky was glowing orange and the ground was very, very hot. Too hot – even for dragons.

But they didn't care. They curled up in a nest of scorching rocks and went to sleep. When they woke their feet and wings were badly singed. 'Ouch, oooh!' they squealed, hopping from foot to foot.

Coming as close as he dared, the Dragon Master asked, 'Can I help?'

But the naughty pair turned their backs on the Dragon Master.

'We don't need him! Let's get a drink and stand in a pond to cool off,' suggested Igneous.

'We'll be fine on our own, *thanks*!' Furnace agreed.

The two dragons dragged themselves through the smoky forest, but their flames had dried all the pools and streams. On and on they trudged, very sore and sorry for themselves.

At last, Igneous whispered, 'I wish the Dragon Master were here.'

'So do I,' Furnace agreed. And they both sat down and cried.

The Dragon Master wasn't far away. When he heard the draggony-blubbing, he came running.

Igneous and Furnace were sitting on their tails and wiping their noses on blistered wings.

'I have an idea,' the Dragon Master said quietly.

The mischief-makers sniffed back tears. 'Ye-es?' they stammered.

'Follow me.' And he led Igneous and Furnace through the silent, ruined forest until they couldn't crawl another step.

Not far off they heard a light, tinkling sound. The Dragon Master led them to a silvery stream that trickled between blackened rocks.

With shouts of delight, the thirsty dragons drank.

When they had finished, the Dragon Master said, 'Better? Good. Now get cracking; bring the forest back.'

'What *us*?' Igneous scowled.

Furnace spread his claws. 'How?'

'Think about it!' The Dragon Master said. And he left them to it.

All day, the dragons cooled their blisters in the stream and sulked. There was still nothing to eat. They couldn't fly to hunt and they were too ashamed to go home.

At last Furnace splashed out of the water. 'Come on,' he said. 'Let's get started.'

For weeks, the dragons cleared the pools and streams and planted and watered little saplings.

They watched with delight as birds and animals slowly returned. When the dragons were sure the

18

forest was repairing itself, they began to make their way back towards Kilve.

It was night when they reached the last great hilltop and looked down on the moonlit coastline. Furnace sat with his tail curled around his feet. 'They'll know all about us…' he whispered. 'Will they want us back?'

Standing next to him, Igneous sighed. 'I want to go home, but I daren't. Let's just *look* at Kilve for a bit.'

And he kicked at a large stone.

That rolled…

And *twitched*.

Igneous picked it up. It was leathery and had a crack in it…

'It's a dragon egg, and it's about to hatch,' Furnace gasped, pulling the shell away.

From inside, a tiny silver claw appeared, then another. A whole arm, a leg, a pointed head, then a thin little body slithered out of its broken prison.

And a tiny baby dragon lay panting on the grass.

Treasure

After their fire games, Igneous and Furnace were too scared to go back to Kilve. Now they were in a real pickle. They had found a baby dragon, newly hatched, and they had no idea how to look after it.

It was a dark, chilly night and there was no one else around to help.

'Ember would know just what to do,' Furnace sighed.

'Ember's in Kilve,' Igneous replied. 'I wish the Dragon Master were here.'

Furnace shook his head. 'He'd only tell us to think. I don't like thinking. It usually means we have to do something we don't like.'

Igneous stared hard at the little baby panting in the grass. 'Does she look a bit odd to you?' he asked.

'It's just the dark,' said Furnace. 'She'll be all right by daylight.'

So they fed the hatchling some crickets and curled around her to keep her warm.

But in the morning they saw the baby had no wings.

'UGH! Tread on her quick!' screamed Furnace.

Igneous felt all sick and cold. He wanted to squash her too. He could say they'd rolled on her by accident while they were asleep.

But the Dragon Master would know it was a lie.

'No,' he said firmly. 'All dragons are precious. And this one needs help quickly. Maybe her wings will grow soon? The Dragon Master will do something. We must take her to Kilve.'

Furnace shuddered. He wasn't ready to go back and he didn't want to touch the 'thing' that lay on the grass. 'You can go. I'm staying here.'

'Well, just help me get started, will you?' asked Igneous picking an empty bird's nest out of a tree. He put it down next to the helpless newborn. 'In you hop,' he said kindly. But she was too weak. Very carefully, he hooked her in with a claw.

'It'll be dead before you get home. It's not worth the effort,' said Furnace sulkily.

'*She'll* be fine if you help. Put the nest up between my wings so I can carry her home. Then you can go back to the forest if you like.'

Wrinkling his nose, Furnace used his claw tips to settle the twiggy cradle onto his friend's back. Igneous started to walk, but the nest kept slipping on the dragon's shiny scales.

'Come with me a bit of the way, just to the edge of Kilve. If she falls from my back it'll kill her.'

Furnace muttered something horrid, but did as he was asked.

Slowly, they swayed their way down the cliff paths and across the bay. Furnace and Igneous felt very scared.

'We can't do this,' Furnace insisted. 'What if they throw rocks at us? The Dragon Master will have told them what we did to the Midnight Forest.'

Igneous was worried too. He looked across to the caves where he could see the older dragons bustling about. 'Perhaps we should wait until dark, then we could sneak in and leave her at Ember's cave.'

Furnace peered into the nest on Igneous's back. 'She's very weak. She mightn't last that long. We've got to keep going.' Then Furnace blushed purple.

Only a few hours before, he'd wanted to tread on the baby. 'Besides,' he blustered, '*you* can't sneak anywhere. Your version of being "quiet" would wake the Nidhogg!'

So they kept going. But as it happened, Furnace and Igneous needn't have worried about the other dragons being cross. Kilve was alive with noise and bustle, and their arrival was ignored.

The day before, Horace had been playing football with Fireworks and Fizzle when their "ball" had started to split! They had been using another dragon egg! After a long search, they had found two more.

Pumice immediately took them all into her cave for safe-keeping. 'Because *I* never play football with my visitors!' she said crustily.

Later that morning, two of the three eggs had hatched.

There was a long, thin girl they called Clarys and a short, fat boy they called Maurice. Their arrival caused such a stir, no one had time to be cross when Igneous and Furnace turned up.

They went to Ember's cave first, but she brushed them aside. 'I'm very busy dears. I'll look at what you've found another time. I'm sure it's very nice, but please keep out of my way today.'

As they stood outside Ember's cave, wondering

what to do, Flamethrower came thudding past. He lowered his head and tutted. 'What are you two doing standing around? There's work to be done! Make yourselves useful!'

Igneous tried to say, 'Please, we need your help,' but the dragon's green-blue tail had already disappeared into the next cave.

Everyone was in a hurry. It was hopeless. How could they get help for this sickly baby dragon?

Miserable and dejected, Igneous and Furnace sat on a rock next to the sea, hugging the nest and its tiny occupant, wondering what to do.

'I'm hungry!' announced Furnace, launching himself into the skies. He soon returned with two fat cod, one for himself and one for Igneous – and a sprat or two for the baby. The big dragons began to enjoy their lunch, but the wingless hatchling just gave a tiny shake and stared at her lunch.

Furnace, with his mouth full of fish, said, 'C'mon 'ittle 'un - s'good for 'oo.'

But she still didn't eat.

'Don't talk with your mouth full!' grumbled Igneous. 'It's a bad example for the baby.' Then very gently, he opened the baby's mouth and pushed her food inside.

She swallowed and blinked her garnet eyes.

'She's taken it! Give her another one, quick!' squealed Furnace delightedly.

Just then a gravelly voice behind them demanded, 'Just what are you two young ruffians up to?'

It was Pumice. That meant trouble.

The two dragons crawled aside and let the dragoness peer into the nest.

Where did you find her?' Pumice growled, glaring at Igneous and Furnace.

'P-p-p-please P-P-Pumice, we found her up on the hillside, late last night. She's poorly and she needs help, but everyone's so busy with the other hatchlings, no one wants to know about her.'

'She's broken you see, she's... she's...' stammered Furnace, staring guiltily at where Pumice's wings had once been.

'I can see exactly what's wrong with her!' roared Pumice. 'Don't just stand there gawping, fetch me whelks and winkles, mussels, anything tiny! And you, the daft-looking one,' she shook a claw at Igneous, 'Warm me a puddle of water if you haven't forgotten how to breathe fire.'

Igneous winced, but Pumice ignored him. 'Fetch the Dragon Master, he's with Fireworks. *Move!*' she roared. Then with a flick of her scaly old tail, she swept the nest and the baby into her cave.

Igneous and Furnace ran to do as they were told. By evening, the little dragon was looking much greener and fatter as she snuggled next to Pumice in the Great Dragon Circle.

First, the Dragon Master called Maurice and Clarys forward and their names were proudly announced with cheers and much rattling of scales. Everyone was very excited. But when the wingless one wriggled forward, there was an embarrassed silence. The other dragons looked away, or tried to persuade Horace that it was bedtime.

The Dragon Master scooped the wingless baby into his arms. 'Who is going to name this dragoness?'

No one spoke.

'Igneous, Furnace, speak up. You found her!' ordered Pumice.

Igneous crawled over and nudged the little one with his nose. Her big eyes glinted back at him with love.

'I name her Treasure. She's the best Treasure a dragon ever had!' he proclaimed loudly.

This time there were cheers, although not many.

Then, from the back, Fawkes yelled, 'But we're not going to keep her, are we? I mean, the great Pumice excepted, what use is a *wingless* dragon?'

This time there were a few murmurs of agreement,

but most of the crowd stayed silent.

The Dragon Master raised an eyebrow at Igneous and Furnace. 'Well?'

Furnace took his place on the other side of Treasure. Eyes blazing, he glared around the Circle. 'Of *course* we're keeping her. Every dragon is precious, even broken ones!'

'But what *use* is she?' demanded Fawkes. 'We'll have to spend all our time looking after her. She'll slow us down. I mean, she'll always be a problem, won't she?'

Igneous could feel his fire rising in fury. But he spoke firmly: 'If it wasn't for her, we would still be out in the Midnight Forest, too afraid to come back. She gave us the courage to return and say we're sorry to everyone.'

Furnace's green and blue scales were bristling with anger. 'And I never realized before that it's nice to do something for someone else. *I* say she stays. She's *our* dragon. The West Wind blew her to us and here she stays because we love her!'

He picked Treasure up and held her tenderly in his claws. She blinked her red eyes, wriggled and burped lovingly up at him.

Furnace smiled, drew a deep breath and added quietly, 'And – and I'm sorry too – for burning down the Midnight Forest.'

The Dragon Master gave the two dragons a proud and pleased hug, as everyone (except Fawkes and one or two others) cheered, roared and rattled their wings until the rocks began to fall.

Dragon Flight

Little Maurice did not like getting into mischief or playing football. He spent all day trying to make his untidy scales lie flat, or admiring himself in rock pools. He never flew more than was necessary because it ruffled his wings and dulled their sheen.

Clarys on the other hand loved football. She also liked to see how high she could fly and how fast she could dive into the wild waves. In the evenings she and Horace would crawl through the wet and filthy tunnels behind the caves so they could bounce out suddenly on unsuspecting dragons, scaring them half to death.

The older dragons were quite shocked!

Pumice was shocked as well, but for a different reason – few of the dragons seemed at all concerned about Treasure. So, old as she was, Pumice looked after her and the last unhatched egg, while Igneous and Furnace caught fish for them all and ran Pumice's errands.

Day after day, Horace and the new babies became long and sleek. Their ruby eyes glinted in the sunlight and their silver claws curved bright and strong.

Horace, Maurice and Clarys loved fishing the wild seas with the older dragons, but Treasure stayed quietly next to Pumice, learning how to make meals and medicines from the different seaweeds.

She learned which rocks, ground into powder, could be used to treat wing-rot, and how to listen to the voices of the wind and sea to hear their weather secrets. Soon she knew when the skies would be calm and when the storms would be too wild for even the bravest dragons to fly.

Treasure was good at learning. She spent long hours with her turquoise tail wrapped carefully around her, so the rougher dragons would not accidentally-on-purpose tread on it when they thumped by. Quietly she watched everything that happened at Kilve until she began to understand things that the others missed completely.

32

The Dragon Master liked talking with Treasure, which made Horace, Maurice and Clarys jealous: not that they could be bothered to spend much time with him. When the Dragon Master gave Treasure a pretty pink stone to wear, Clarys and Maurice were furious.

'Look, there she goes,' muttered Clarys between her teeth, 'she thinks she's so special. Dragon Master's pet! It's not fair!' Clarys knew she was being silly. She liked jewels but never wore them. They got in the way when she was crawling underground.

Horace scowled. 'Treasure can't fly, how can she know when it's going to rain or when the cod are shoaling? She goes on about smelling the wind changing... But it's all rubbish.'

Maurice was smoothing his wayward scales. 'Treasure's scales always look glossy. I wish she wasn't here at all,' he added quietly.

The others looked at him.

A gleam came into Horace's eyes. A nasty smirk hovered at the corner of Clarys's mouth. 'There is that rocky island in the middle of the sea to the north. She can smell the wind as much as she likes there.'

'So, we wouldn't *hurt* her?' Horace asked.

'Of *course* not!' the others chimed in.

Maurice grinned, 'So we'd just put her on her own island where she can do all her special smelling and listening without…'

'*Us* getting in her way!' Clarys added slyly.

That afternoon, the sea breezes were gentle and the sky was a lovely deep blue. Clarys brought Treasure some fish. She had a lovely smile on her face but her fangs showed just a little. 'We've been thinking, *dear* Treasure, that it can't be fun, never flying, so Maurice, Horace and I are going to take you for a little flight – wouldn't that be nice?'

Treasure tried to say, 'Thank you, but I'm not worried about not flying, I'm quite happy as I am,' but the fish was particularly large, so it came out as 'angoo, u-I'm so eawy urry agout iyig.'

Then a bone caught in her throat, so she couldn't shout for help when Horace (who was quite a big dragon by now) swooped down, grabbed her with his claws and swung her up into the cloudless sky.

In desperation, Treasure spat the fish out and screamed, but they were too far away for anyone to hear.

She wriggled in Horace's talons and shouted: 'Be careful! The weather's going to change, you mustn't fly high today!'

Clarys flapped next to Treasure and grinned. 'Don't be silly. It's a beautiful day, not a cloud in the sky. You don't understand flying like we do. Don't be scared, we're looking after you!'

And to prove the point, Horace let go of Treasure, but she didn't fall far before Clarys's silver claws grabbed her middle.

What are they plotting? Treasure thought. *Clarys and Horace are strong, fast flyers, but Maurice never flies further than he has to.*

Treasure tried not to show her fear. She sniffed the wind. The air was crackling and somewhere in the distance she could hear thunder rolling. A big storm was coming – why couldn't the others smell it too? They mustn't play pranks today of all days!

The wind grew cold and changed direction, plunging them into a huge grey cloud. Heavy drops of rain landed on their noses, followed by lightening and thunder. A sudden squall buffeted them from side to side, until poor Treasure, dangling by her middle, began to feel very sick. She had only ever been taken for low flights by fat old Fizzle.

'Can't fly in a storm like this!' Clarys gasped as she passed Treasure back to Horace. 'Must go home!'

Horace shook water from his wings and banked to the side, but a new blast of wind tossed him upside down and he almost dropped Treasure. Clarys and Maurice squealed as they span out of control. They could not turn back. The storm was too strong, even for full-size dragon wings.

And they were being blown steadily away from Kilve.

The little dragons struggled on, looking for somewhere to land, but there was only endless sea. Water seeped under Maurice's scales. His wings sagged and he sank until he was barely skimming the lashing waves. He was very frightened. Horace and Clarys were coping a little better, but passing Treasure between them like a bundle of wet seaweed was making them all tired. None of them could keep going much longer.

Horace was all for dropping Treasure into the sea. 'No one would blame us. We might just make it on our own.'

Clarys snatched Treasure back. 'She didn't ask to be brought with us. Are you going to tell the Dragon Master where his beloved Treasure is?'

Horace saw the point and shut up.

At last, Maurice spotted a tall, grey pinnacle standing high above the raging seas. There was not much room, but it was better than nothing.

Flying lower, Clarys circled and dropped Treasure gently. The others landed nearby, then very carefully they crawled across the slimy stone until they found a crevice that was deep enough to hide them all.

As darkness fell, the shivering dragons huddled together and cried. It was a miserable night. The thunderous crashing of waves made their shelter shudder. As the tide rose, spray lashed their refuge, showering them with icy water and stones.

The next day the wind dropped and the sun began to shine.

Horace, Maurice and Clarys climbed out and spread their wings to dry. Lower down, Treasure stretched on a rocky shelf to warm her flaking scales.

They were all very hungry, but the foaming tide still flung itself against broken granite teeth below. Fishing was far too dangerous.

Treasure listened to the hopeless dragons discussing their plight and felt sorry for them. Slowly and clumsily she scrambled lower until she found purple lava weed left by the tide. It tasted faintly fishy so with a few gull eggs, it was a tasty snack.

Carefully she gathered a large bundle of the weed and carried it back up to the others in her mouth. It took her the best part of the morning to gather enough. At first Maurice and Horace refused to eat, saying it was 'muck!' but Maurice shut up when he caught the warning look in Clarys's eye. Before long, even fussy Horace was munching heartily.

Treasure was worried. She could tell by the stars

that they were a long way from home. Horace had a torn wing, she'd wrapped it in healing weeds, but he wouldn't be able to fly properly for several days. They were all hungry, cold and weak. Worst of all, although the wind had dropped, she could smell new storms brewing. Things looked bad. The others depended on her, whether they liked it or not.

While the dragons dozed after their meal, Treasure slipped away to listen to the West Wind as the Dragon Master had taught her, and a plan unfolded in her head.

'I must hurry this lull won't last long,' Treasure told herself. 'I could do with help, but the others need to build up their strength. I'll have to do this alone.'

Laboriously, Treasure climbed down to where the morning's high tide had dumped driftwood and dried seaweed. She collected as much as she could in her mouth, then climbed back up to the top and started to pile it neatly. Up and down, all afternoon until she ached in every bone and joint.

'I wish I could rest, I'm so tired,' she sighed, 'but I daren't. The next storm is almost here.'

By evening, the bonfire was quite big.

Horace woke first. 'What's that for? Are we roasting a shark tonight?' he asked hopefully.

Clarys opened her eyes and glared at him.

'Whatever she's doing you could at least help!' she snapped. Spreading her wings, she swooped down to the high tide mark and grabbed some heavy branches.

Horace and Maurice ignored the girls and went fishing.

'It's getting dark, don't go far!' Treasure warned, but the seas were rough and they came back very quickly. Horace grudgingly tossed a crab at Treasure's feet and he went off on his own to munch his catch.

'So what *are* you up to?' Clarys asked with a mouthful of supper. 'Got the tidy-up bug and trying to keep the seas clean?'

'You'll see!' Treasure smiled.

When they had finished eating, Treasure asked Clarys to blow fire onto the heap of wood. Soon a great blaze lit the sky for miles. Maurice and Horace felt cheered by the sight of flames and they fetched a tree trunk that had been too heavy for Clarys.

The night was long and dark. By dawn, both the fire and Treasure's hopes were getting low, when they heard a shout in the skies.

In the glow of sunrise they saw a flight of dragons swooping towards them. And on the back of Flamethrower was the Dragon Master.

The little dragons jumped up and roared, belching flames in delight. The rescuers circled and landed, just as Treasure's bonfire crumbled to ashes.

The Dragon Master hugged them all, especially his little Treasure.

Clarys, who was crying hard, came and hugged Treasure too. 'Thank you for saving us. How did you know to light a fire?' she asked. 'We all thought you were daft!'

Treasure shrugged and smiled. 'I knew the grown-ups would come for us as soon as the wind dropped. We just had to make sure they found us.'

Why?

As the last egg hatched, a tiny turquoise snout pushed into the world and *trouble* began.

Old Pumice, who'd been watching, pulled bits of shell from the baby's shiny scales. 'Hello, dear,' she smiled. 'Time to come out now.'

The baby stretched his wings and shook himself. '*Why?*' he asked in a cheeky little voice.

Pumice had never been asked that before. She sat back on her hind legs and scratched her head. 'Well, dear, you're ready, done, made... er...'

The baby wriggled and blinked his ruby eyes. '*Why?*' he piped once more.

Pumice stroked his head with a gentle claw. 'You

see, a long time ago, a Mummy dragon laid your egg. You've been growing slowly for a long time, and now you're much too big for your shell.' Pumice smiled. She was pleased with that answer.

'Why?' came the persistent squeak.

Now Pumice was getting cross. 'Come on, dear, it's time for tea.'

'Why?'

'You must be hungry!'

The baby looked interested. 'Yes, I am. Why am I?'

'Because your tummy's empty, dear, you've never had any tea before.'

'Why?'

Pumice huffed. 'Because we couldn't get fish through the shell to you.'

'Why?'

'Because it wouldn't go.'

'Why?'

By this time old Pumice had had enough. With firm claws, she took the new baby to see Flamethrower, the biggest dragon at Kilve.

'Here!' Pumice announced. 'The last one's hatched. He's a bit of a Bright Spark; maybe we should call him Sparky for short? He's impossible! You'd better find someone better-tempered than me to look after him!'

'Why?' asked Sparky, looking innocently from

dragon to dragon with his gleaming little eyes.

'He does that all the time,' said Pumice. 'Whatever you say, he interrupts with "*why*?"'

Perhaps his voice is stuck,' said Flamethrower kindly. The huge, green dragon lifted the little one onto a rock, so he could get a better look at him.

'Now, can you say my name, "Flame-thrower"?'

'Why?' asked Sparky.

'Well, I want to see if your voice is stuck.'

'Why?'

'Well, if your voice is stuck, you'll need a doctor but if you're just being rude, you'll need to be told off and probably sent to bed!' Flamethrower frowned.

'...*Why*?' came the reply.

'So we can make sure you grow up into a good dragon,' explained Flamethrower patiently.

'Why?'

'Because that's the right thing to do.'

'Why?'

'Because that's the way the West Wind blows.'

'Why?'

Flamethrower was getting very cross. 'Because if you aren't good, the Nidhogg will come and get you!'

Sparky opened his eyes wide, but he wasn't the least bit scared. 'Why?'

Flamethrower gritted his long fangs and muttered,

43

'You're quite right, Pumice. Let's try taking him to Fireworks. He knows the answer to everything. We've got to do something before... I lose... my... *temper*!'

'Why?' persisted the cheeky baby as he trotted after them.

But Pumice and Flamethrower ignored him as they climbed the rocky path to the clever dragon's home.

Just then, there was the most terrific *crash* and purple smoke belched out of the cave. Fireworks staggered out, covered in soot and very pleased with himself. 'I did it!' he beamed. 'I've made purple fire for the Dragon Master's birthday – he *will* be pleased!'

'Why?' came the inevitable squeak.

Fireworks peered down through the smoke at the baby dragon.

'Who, may I ask, is this?'

'Sparky' said Flamethrower.

'*Bright* Sparky,' added Pumice. 'He's impossible! He wants to know "why?" about everything, and we just can't cope!'

Fireworks shook his head. 'Well, well, we must let the little ones explore and discover, otherwise they never learn, do they? All they need is a good teacher and a little patience. Give him to me, and I'll sort him out!'

'But *why*?' squeaked Sparky as he was led by the

claws into an untidy cave.

Next morning, an exhausted and dull-eyed Fireworks crawled into the sunlight and blinked wearily. Sparky trotted after him, test tube in one claw and a bag of yellow powder in the other.

'But why can't I put this in here, Fireworks, *why*?'

'Because I've told you, it will go bang!'

'I like bangs!'

'I don't!' said Fireworks.

'Yes you do! Yes you do!' squealed Sparky, jumping up and down with glee on Fireworks's back. 'You told me so last night!'

'Yes, but I don't like bangs *all* the time!' moaned the exhausted dragon.

'Why?'

'Because they make my head ache.'

'Why?'

'The noise makes my brain rattle.'

'Why?'

'Because it just *does*!'

'Why?'

Fireworks groaned, covered his sore head with his wings and shuddered.

Just to be sure of 'Why?' Sparky tipped a little yellow powder into the test tube. He laughed with glee at the terrific *BANG!* that shook the cliffs. All the dragons came running, hopping and flying, certain that the whole of Kilve beach was tumbling into the sea.

Flamethrower and Pumice scooped Sparky off to the cave of Fizzle, a delightful but totally deaf old dragon. He was everyone's friend, but never had the faintest idea what was going on because he was too busy eating to learn lip-reading or sign language.

After a packet or two of his best chocolate biscuits, Fizzle understood that young Sparky needed a home, just until things could be sorted out a bit. Fizzle nodded happily and made up a cosy seaweed bed. Every time Sparky asked 'why?' Fizzle just grinned and handed the young rascal another biscuit.

This arrangement went on happily for weeks. Sparky still wanted to know 'why' about everything, but the dragons didn't mind because Fizzle was very good at getting Sparky in bed on time, so their evenings were peaceful.

One day, after finding out why rocks were heavy and the wind was light, then discussing why the sky was blue and why fish tasted nice, Sparky was sharing Fizzle's chocolate biscuits when the Dragon Master came to call.

'Well, young dragon, are you ready to start your first flying lessons?'

Sparky spread his fine shiny wings and considered them. 'Why?'

'Because you're big enough to learn now.'

'Why?'

'Because you've got to learn to go fishing for yourself.'

'Why?'

'Because you're a big dragon now.'

'Why?'

'Because you eat too many chocolate biscuits.'

'Why?'

'That,' said the Dragon Master seriously, 'is a very good question.' He stroked his long white beard and thought. 'In fact, you may be almost too big to learn to fly. Perhaps you ought to visit my wise friend, the golden dragon of the Midnight Forest.'

Ignoring the usual endless string of questions, the Dragon Master told Sparky to say 'Goodbye and thank you for having me,' very clearly to Fizzle, and they set off.

They walked through the tall, dark trees. Sparky was scared, but when something caught his eye, he couldn't resist asking questions. At last he knew the differences between mushrooms and toadstools, foxes and foxgloves, mountains and molehills.

In a sunny clearing they found a small, golden

dragon asleep on a stone. As the visitors approached, the dragon opened his emerald eyes, uncurled his snaky body and pushed his head into the Dragon Master's hand. 'Greetings,' he said softly. 'Who is your young friend?'

'This,' said the Dragon Master, 'is an inquisitive little chap called Sparky. We'd be very grateful if he could live with you for a few days. He needs *educating*!'

Sparky was horrified. He did not want to live with a golden stranger in the middle of a darksome wood. He would miss all his friends and the sea.

'Er... Why?' he asked, but rather uncertainly this time.

The golden dragon stretched his claws and shrugged, then with a wink and a raised eyebrow, he simply asked, 'Why not?'

Sparky was so amazed he opened his mouth...

Then he shut it again. He couldn't think of an answer.

Why Not?

Sparky was a friendly little dragon, but very cheeky and rather lazy. He always wanted to know 'why?' about everything, but he never stopped to actually listen to the answers.

In the end, the Dragons of Kilve couldn't cope, so the Dragon Master took Sparky to live with the wise golden dragon of the Midnight Forest. When Sparky asked him 'why?' the golden dragon simply replied, 'Why not?'

Sparky eyed the golden dragon very suspiciously – and the golden dragon just chuckled.

The Dragon Master patted Sparky on his head. 'He needs to learn quite a few "why nots?" I'm afraid,' he

49

said solemnly. 'I'll be back for him soon. He must start flying lessons before he gets too big for his wings. Please do what you can.'

The golden dragon scratched his chin. 'Humm. This won't be easy, but I'll try. Farewell.' Then with a flick of his gleaming tail, he swept out of sight behind his rock.

Sparky tried to run after the Dragon Master, but he had already gone. For the first time in his life, Sparky felt really scared, alone with a stranger in the darksome forest. He sat on the leafy ground and thought, which was something he'd never tried before!

Which way had the Dragon Master gone?

Why had he hurried away without even saying goodbye?

Where was the path through the forest?

Sparky realised he'd been so busy asking questions, he'd noticed nothing about the way they had come – apart from the red toadstools which he now knew were definitely not for eating…

He got to his feet and looked around. There were red toadstools everywhere! How he wished he hadn't talked non-stop all the way! Tears stung his eyes. He tried not to cry but he couldn't help himself.

When Sparky ran out of tears, his fear turned into

crossness. 'Why? Why? *Why*?' he yelled into the trees, stamping hard with his knobbly feet.

At this, a gentle voice behind him said, 'I'm afraid my young friend, that only you can answer that.'

Sparky jumped. The golden dragon was curled on his rock again, smiling through small, pointed teeth. 'It's getting late. Are you coming inside, or are you going to blub out there all night?' he asked.

Sparky looked up through the trees. The sky was turning red. He didn't fancy being outside in the dark, surrounded by woods and all sorts of strange creatures. There was nothing for it but to follow as the golden dragon slipped from his rock and crawled under swaying creepers and ferns.

Inside the cave was cool and dark, but smaller than any of the dragon homes at Kilve.

'Please get some wood from the pile at the back and light a fire,' said the golden dragon.

'Why should I?' Sparky pouted.

The golden dragon shrugged. 'You'll see why.' Then he curled up on a wide rocky shelf and went to sleep.

Sparky tried to do the same, but the night was cold and filled with strange sounds. The moon rose and wolves came sniffing at the cave mouth. Sparky blew a few short blasts of flame at the intruders, but without the space to beat his wings, he couldn't blow much.

By dawn, a grey and exhausted young Sparky understood that a fire would have warmed him as well as keeping nosy neighbours away.

'Time for breakfast,' the golden dragon announced as he wandered into the morning sunlight and stretched his wings.

Sparky looked enthusiastically around him for piles of fresh-caught fish. But there was nothing. 'Excuse me,' he asked as politely as possible, 'but where is breakfast, please?'

'In the woods, of course,' the golden dragon replied, setting off between the trees at a brisk pace.

Sparky had to trot hard to keep up. The forest was very dense and difficult for a large young dragon who was used to open spaces. Soon, they came to a clearing. There, the golden dragon lay on his belly and signalled to Sparky to do the same.

As they watched, a family of rabbits came out to graze.

With a sudden flash of a claw, a young buck lay dead. Sparky watched in dumb amazement.

The golden dragon began to gnaw the rabbit, then he stopped and smiled at Sparky. 'Aren't you going to catch one?' he asked.

'I... I... I've never caught a rabbit before,' he muttered. The truth was, he'd never caught anything before.

'Oh, it's quite easy,' the golden dragon assured him. 'The trick is in being so still they forget you're there. Then *zap*! He's yours. Mmmm, delicious!' Then he added thoughtfully, 'But we won't take any more from this clearing. A few here and a few there, that's the rule.'

At last Sparky dared to ask, 'Er... Why?'

The golden dragon smiled. 'Because if we eat them all, it'll be a long time before there're any rabbits here again.'

'I... I don't think I fancy rabbit. I think the fur might get stuck in my fangs.'

'Of course, you're a sea dragon. There's a river nearby. Perhaps you fancy some fish?'

Sparky cheered up immediately and trotted after his beautiful host. Soon they were squatting by the glittering water as it danced its way to the sea.

Sparky looked at his new friend expectantly.

'Well... I'll leave you to it, shall I?' the golden dragon smiled, then he slid back into the dark shadows of the forest and was gone.

Sparky looked at the water in dismay. He'd never caught a fish before, either. He stamped his foot.

'*WHY*? It's just not fair!' he screamed.

But the forest didn't answer him.

By noon, the sun was warming Sparky's back. He had slept a little and now he was thirsty as well as hungry. He lay on the riverbank and took a long drink. There were a few small fish and after a great deal of effort, he managed to lap a few up with his tongue. But the taste made him hungrier than ever. He rested his head on his claws and looked longingly to where fat brown trout poked up their speckled heads and made gentle plopping sounds as they caught insects.

'If only I could fly,' thought Sparky. 'I'd skim the water gracefully and catch trout like Horace does.' He stretched his wings, examined them and folded them up. The thought of flying made him nervous.

'But I really don't understand why the golden dragon doesn't feed me. The others always did. Why did the Dragon Master leave me here like this? *Why*? And tears trickled down his nose again.

Sparky's tummy rumbled on, so he waded into the river and pounced on a fat fish. But it wriggled away, laughing bubbles at him.

As the day cooled, Sparky looked around and noticed a few chestnuts. Lightly toasted in dragonfire they were better than nothing.

As the sun began to sink, he was getting worried, for the golden dragon didn't come back. What if he'd forgotten? Sparky had tried to watch the way they'd come, but the paths between the shadowy trees all looked the same. He could not remember the way back.

So Sparky began to heap up dried wood. He didn't fancy a night on his own, but if it had to be done, he'd have the biggest bonfire ever seen in the Midnight Forest (apart from Igneous and Furnace's of course).

But Sparky needn't have feared, for the golden dragon arrived before darkness fell. He smiled approvingly at the wood waiting to be lit.

'Good, I'm glad to see you've been busy. Did you eat well?' he asked. Then ignoring the list of Sparky's woes, he took a large bundle of sticks from the heap. 'We won't be able to carry all of this, but we'll fetch the rest tomorrow.'

Then without so much as a glance over his shoulder, the golden dragon disappeared into the darkening shadows.

Sparky scooped up as much wood as he could carry and staggered down the path behind him.

That night, the fire at the cave entrance burned and crackled. No wolves came prowling and if Sparky hadn't been so hungry, he would have slept very well.

The next day, Sparky was left by the river to catch his breakfast once more. As soon as the dragon's golden tail had disappeared, Sparky waded out into the shallows and wondered why the fish darted away as soon as he got into the water. He thought a little and realised that fish might behave like rabbits. If he stayed very still, they might come back, then he could grab something bigger than a minnow.

His plan worked well and he was munching his second medium-sized trout when the golden dragon appeared and told him to hurry, for it was time to go.

'Why?' Sparky demanded irritably.

The golden dragon shrugged in his usual way. 'You'll see,' he said and walked off.

Sparky went back to catching fish. Now he was getting good at it, he didn't want to stop. He didn't notice the sky getting dark until large, sploshy drops of rain landed on his nose. And he was alone again.

'I should have followed the golden dragon straight away and worried about "why?" later,' he muttered crossly as he stomped homewards with the rain clattering on his scales. Then he came to a choice of paths. Which one should he take? That morning he really had watched and not talked, but the forest looked different in the rain.

He stopped and looked around. Then he saw claw

and tail marks in the mud. That way!

At last, extremely wet and miserable, Sparky reached the golden dragon's cave. Gratefully, he stretched out by the roaring fire. Steam curled off his scales and he slept.

When he awoke, there was a packet of chocolate biscuits right by his nose. He sat up.

'Hello,' said a familiar voice. On the other side of the fire sat the Dragon Master wrapped in his starry cloak. He held out his hands and Sparky crawled over and nuzzled his best friend joyfully.

'Are you ready to come home now?' the Dragon Master asked gently.

Sparky looked up with twinkling eyes and grinned. With a glance at the golden dragon, he winked and laughed.

'Why not?'

Nasty Dreams

Long summer evenings are perfect for dragon-play.

Lively youngsters spiral high in the warm skies, then drop like stones on the lazy ones floating below. This leads to furious chases to the rocky pinnacles, then diving competitions for crunchy lobsters deep under the green waters.

After one such evening, the light lingered and none of the young dragons felt sleepy. They lit a bonfire of driftwood in a cave, ate roast shark and sang silly songs until dark fell at last.

It was then that Treasure asked, 'Who'd like to hear about Leviathan?'

'Yes please!' chorused the others.

There were many things Treasure could not do because she was wingless, but she was a brilliant storyteller.

'As you know,' she began, 'Leviathan is the great sea serpent who's twisted herself right around the world. When she was young, she ate nearly every fish in the sea. The few that were left hid well out of reach. Leviathan became so hungry she swung her black-and-green-fringed jaws over the land, to see what else might be for lunch. She ate anything: lions, sheep, wild boar... even a dragon or two.'

At this, Maurice cuddled up to Clarys.

Treasure went on. 'At last, all the animals fled in terror to the highest point of the world. There, they called as loudly as they could to the Keeper of all Beasts to seal the monster's mouth.

'And the Keeper came. Very firmly, he tied Leviathan's jaws with the wispy end of the serpent's own tail. The unhappy beast could now only suck in a few shrimps, or maybe a very *small* dragon,' she added mischievously as the others huddled wide-eyed around the fire.

When she had finished, Horace piped up: 'Once I chased my own tail for an hour. I thought it was Leviathan's!'

Everyone laughed and Clarys snorted, 'Typical!' Then she added, 'Has anyone heard about the fearsome old wizard who lives at the North Pole? He freezes dragons' wings so they can't ever fly again.'

The others shook their heads. Clarys rolled her eyes in the firelight. 'His captives stay as the wizard's ice statues... *forever!*' she whispered.

Maurice held Horace's claw. Horace gulped, then said, 'Did I ever tell you about the day I swallowed a whole clam and...'

Maurice and Clarys promptly sat on him. 'Yes!' she snapped. 'We *all* know that one!' Then she turned to Treasure. 'Tell us how Pumice lost her wings, I heard there was a great battle?'

'No,' Treasure replied firmly.

'Why?' piped up Sparky.

'Because Pumice has never told me. That's why. In fact, I don't think she's told *anyone* what really happened. Only the Dragon Master knows.'

'Tell us another story then,' Sparky suggested. 'One you made up – I like those.'

'Let me think.' Treasure shivered in the night air.

The dragons pulled another pile of driftwood onto the fire. Black shadows danced up the cave walls. Everything was silent, except for the crackle of the flames and the sighing sea outside.

Then very softly, Treasure began a new tale about an evil little witch who lived all alone in the depths of the Midnight Forest. 'Indeed,' said Treasure, 'it's because of her that it is called the Midnight Forest, for where she dwells, no sunlight ever comes, nor will it until the end of time.'

Treasure's story got longer and longer and spookier and spookier, until the dragons were so scared they hardly dared to breathe.

When it was finished no one spoke.

At last, Clarys whispered, 'I... I think I might just curl up here for the night. I'm too tired to walk back to my cave.' Really, she was too scared to go out into the night in case the witch was hiding in a shadow, waiting for a juicy dragon supper.

Sparky snuggled up to Clarys. 'Can I stay with you?' he asked.

Then, in a very trembly voice, Maurice suggested, 'It'd be fun to spend the night by the fire, instead of going home.'

Treasure got up and went to the cave mouth. She frowned into the dark night. 'I really ought to be going home,' she said. 'Pumice isn't feeling well.'

Then her heart started to pound, for a rocky shadow was slowly shifting quietly up the beach towards them. *The witch!* she thought. *She's real! She's here!* Treasure had a very strange feeling in her tummy. She was beginning to wish she hadn't told that last story.

'I don't think Pumice will mind if I don't go back,' Treasure added quietly. 'I've slept out before. On warm nights.'

'But this isn't warm!' said Maurice glumly. 'I'm frozen!'

'There's plenty of wood at the back,' said Clarys.

Horace shuddered as he stared at a deep black gash of a shadow that ran between him and the woodpile. He wondered if it was really a bottomless pit? *How deep is bottomless?* he wondered.

'Perhaps we should just snuggle up a bit closer?' suggested Treasure, trying to keep warm against Maurice's scratchy scales.

At last, everyone fell silent, listening until their ears ached for the tiny footfall of a hungry Forest Witch. No one dared move.

The fire burned lower and lower, until there was just a pile of grey and red ash, but the dragons were all too scared to cross the black shadow to get more wood.

At last, they fell into a doze.

Until…

Crack! A stone knocked against a rock.

All the dragons jerked awake, wide-eyed and rigidly still.

'Wassat?' whispered Clarys.

They all held their breath and shivered.

Another stone. A crunching footfall.

There it was again!

The tread was far too light to be Ember or Flamethrower. Terrified, the dragons screwed up their bright little eyes – so they missed the look of amazement on the Dragon Master's face as he peered into the cave.

'What are you all doing here? The others are worried sick about you!' he said, ducking the overhanging rocks to come inside.

At the sound of his voice, the little dragons squealed and ran to hug him.

The Dragon Master stroked their scales gently. 'What's the matter? You're all so cold but you've been sweating. Are you ill?'

'It's my fault,' Treasure piped up, her voice squeakier than usual. 'I was telling scary stories, then they seemed to come real. I didn't mean to frighten anyone,' she added sadly. 'It started out as fun.'

'And now we're all too scared to go back to our caves,' admitted Horace.

The Dragon Master chewed his white beard

thoughtfully and sat down. 'Put some more wood on the fire, Maurice,' he said.

Maurice looked doubtfully towards the back of the cave. The shadow didn't look quite so 'bottomless' with the Dragon Master here, but he still jumped over it, just in case.

When the fire was blazing and everyone had stopped shivering, the Dragon Master held up his cloak of stars. 'Would you like me to help you sleep now? I'll tell the others you're safe.'

'Oh no!' said Clarys quickly, then not wishing to seem ungrateful, she added, 'We'd like to, but you see, we daren't sleep. Not properly. We keep getting nasty dreams.'

'About the wizard from the north,' said Sparky.

'Mine's about the little witch of the Midnight Forest,' added Maurice.

'And she's coming to get me first because I made her up!' Treasure sobbed.

'I see,' said the Dragon Master kindly. 'Why don't you tell me all about these dreams, then we can see what can be done?'

The Dragon Master spread his cloak on the ground and his friends cuddled up next to him and told their stories. Horace even insisted on telling his tale about his tail. This made the others cross, but the Dragon

Master laughed and scratched Horace's ears.

When they had finished, the little dragons felt much better. Next to their best friend in the bright firelight, the stories lost their scariness.

The Dragon Master stroked their wings. 'You see, it often helps to get your fears out in the open,' he smiled.

Treasure pushed her head under the Dragon Master's arm and looked up at him with wide eyes. 'But I'm not just scared about the witch in my story, I know that was just pretend. It's something else. I don't even know what I'm scared of, but it just sort of creeps all over me and it won't go away.'

The Dragon Master looked serious, then he nodded. 'Then what you must do, is imagine the worst bits of your fears.'

'Must I?' shivered Treasure.

'Trust me,' he said, cuddling her tightly. Then he rolled the little dragons gently onto the floor and held up his cloak.

There were no stars twinkling there now. Just empty blackness.

'Now, make the nasty things come out of your heads and walk into this.'

'How?' they asked.

'Just imagine them. It's quite safe. I'm here.'

And so they all held claws and closed their eyes.

The cloak trembled in the Dragon Master's hands, and then it hung loose. 'Is that everything?' he asked.

They nodded, but Treasure took a deep breath and the cloth shook once more. 'That's it,' she said at last.

The Dragon Master gathered up his cloak and shook it over the fire. Dust, sticks and all sorts of rubbish tumbled into the flames from the black folds.

'There, all gone!' he said.

The little dragons sighed and sagged into a big huddle on the floor.

But the Dragon Master hadn't finished. 'Now and most importantly, we must put something nice in the space where the scariness was, otherwise the nasties might come back.'

Crinkling the corners of his kind eyes, the Dragon Master took a jar of spicy-smelling ointment from his pocket and gently rubbed a little onto each dragon's nose. As he did so, he whispered, 'Think about diving for lobsters and flying in sunshine. Float on the West Wind and you will have quiet dreams. If nasty thoughts come creeping back, call me. I'll be here.'

Then the Dragon Master pulled his cloak of stars over the little dragons and they slept until the morning sun caught in their eyes.

'Beautifulling' Mud

Maurice had a problem. He had no sense of humour. If anyone made a joke about him, he sulked for days.

This was unfortunate because Sparky's favourite game was to see how many tricks he could play on Maurice, before Maurice realized he was being teased.

One day Maurice was dozily flying in the sunshine with one eye open for a fishy snack, when someone's sharp nose rudely poked him in the ribs.

It was Sparky, puffing and panting, as if he'd been flying for hours on his fat little wings. 'Maurice,' he called out, 'do slow down, I've been trying to find you all morning! I've got some exciting news! Clarys and I have discovered magic mud!'

'Magic mud?' Maurice dipped one wing and banked towards Sparky. 'What sort of magic mud? Does it grow nice fat cod? Or maybe it sings when you can't get to sleep?'

'No, no! Nothing like that! It's *beautifulling* mud!' Sparky exclaimed.

'What are you talking about?'

'If you wallow in it and let it dry, then when it cracks off, your scales are all shiny and sparkly!'

Now Maurice's other problem was that he was vain. His scales were always dull and rough, as if he'd been cave-crawling with Clarys. He used loads of scale-polish, but it did no good.

Maurice thought hard. He didn't trust Sparky, but he daren't miss the very slim chance that for once he might be telling the truth. Maurice flapped his wings and slowed a little. 'So how does "beautifulling" mud work?' he asked carefully, not wishing to sound too interested.

The only way Sparky could keep himself from giggling and going purple was to look really excited. 'Who cares? What does it matter? It just makes you beautifuller! Come and see!' Then jiggling up and down with glee, the naughty dragon flew away. And

Maurice couldn't help but follow him to where a shallow river shimmered into the sea.

There the slimy water oozed its way between a few hillocks of rough grass.

A great place for wading birds – and a very bad place for dragons!

At last Sparky nudged Maurice's tail. 'Look! Down there, it's Clarys.'

Basking in the sun at the edge of a muddy island was Clarys. Her blue-green scales gleamed as if she had been oiling them for days, and when she waved her silver claws flashed and caught the light. As Maurice and Sparky approached, she stretched her wings to show off their delicate webs.

'Oh!' exclaimed Maurice, wheeling into land, 'You're beautiful!'

Clarys, who really didn't care two hoots about her looks, put her head on one side and smiled. 'Thank you Maurice. Why don't you try the mud? It's lovely and cool. It'll make your scales just like mine.'

Maurice landed next to Clarys and narrowed his ruby eyes. Was that a giggle playing at the corners of her mouth? She wasn't looking him straight in the eye, was it because the sun was too bright?

He flicked out his tongue and tasted the mud on the ground. It was sour and greasy. Could it really have made her scales so shiny and colourful? There wasn't a trace of slime on her.

He wasn't sure. Slowly he walked around Clarys, inspecting her carefully.

Sparky, who was aching with the effort of not laughing, sat and watched.

At last Maurice perched near the edge of the mud and dangled the tip of his tail into the stinking black sludge. 'Ugh!' he squealed, whipping his tail back. 'I don't believe you! This is horrid stuff. I'm going home.'

Ooze dripped everywhere as he clambered to his feet. His claws slipped and with a pitiful howl he tumbled down the rocks into the stinking gunge below.

Slop! Slurp! *Splat*!

Terrified, Maurice floundered wildly. Splashes of mud smothered Clarys and Sparky from head to claw.

'Yuck! *Stoppit*!' They screamed with disgust.

Then out from the slime oozed a greeny-blackish shape. Slowly and nastily it slithered up the shore. From under the dripping goo, Maurice's angry red eyes glowered at Clarys and Sparky.

The two little dragons were not laughing now.

Slowly they backed away from the terrible monster that was coming to get them.

But they weren't fast enough.

Suddenly, Maurice bellowed and shook himself hard, splattering mud everywhere. It trickled down snouts, into eyes, over tongues and along backs. Now all three of them were cold, wet and miserable. But worst of all, the mud was all over their wings! Now, dragons can only fly if their wings are kept absolutely clean. If the webs are torn or wet, flight is difficult, but if they get muddy – it is impossible.

At first, the three little dragons stared at each other in silent rage.

'Now look at what you've done!' muttered Maurice, snorting enormous green bubbles through his nose as he spoke.

'*You're* the clumsy oaf!' roared Clarys, 'How did we know you'd dance around like a hippo? It's not our fault you fell in!'

'But you were *trying* to get me in, weren't you?' Maurice took a threatening step towards the others.

'Not really, no!' She kept her claws crossed because she was lying.

'I've a good mind to push you two right in and hold you under for a week!' roared Maurice, although he was trying hard not to cry.

Round and round they went, shouting and stamping, until the wind blew cold and the sun began to redden and sink in the west.

'It'll be dark soon,' Sparky said. 'Hadn't we better get back? If we keep on like this, we'll be stuck out here all night.'

The other two stopped arguing.

'You're right,' Clarys replied. 'Let's find some clean water and get this muck off, then we'll be able to fly.'

Sulky and silent, the three dragons picked their way across the tussocky mudflats towards home. It was getting darker and the incoming tide was sweeping towards them, but it was very muddy and no good for washing.

At last the dragons became stranded on a little reedy island with no hope of getting any further that night. There wasn't much room, but they were all too angry to snuggle up. Instead they glared at each other miserably.

Clarys was cross with Sparky for having thought up the daft idea in the first place, and she was irritated with Maurice for spraying her with mud.

Sparky was particularly angry with Clarys for insisting on going to the mudflats – a very long way from home.

Although Maurice was furious with the other two, mostly he blamed himself for being stupid enough to have listened to Sparky and envied Clarys.

It was a long, cold night.

When the wind became really bitter, a few 'I'm sorrys,' were whispered and they curled up closer and felt warmer. But not much. Rising water hissed through the reeds until there was so little room, they had to let their tails dangle in icy wetness.

'Do you know what?' asked Clarys at last.

'What?' muttered an unhappy Maurice.

'I can't decide if the Dragon Master is the first or last person I want to see right now.'

'Me too,' moaned Sparky. 'If he was here, everything would be all right. But when I *do* see him I'll run and hide... because of what we've been up to.'

There was silence, then from a little way off a kindly voice spoke in the darkness: 'Please make up your minds, young dragons. Do you want me or not? I'm freezing over here.'

'*Dragon Master!*' they shouted, scrambling and slipping over each other. 'We do want you! We're here!'

The Dragon Master lit a glow of light on the end of his staff and he began to pick his way through the marshes towards them. 'Don't move, I'll come to you,' he called out. 'Will someone lend me a tail?'

Clarys was nearest. She wriggled her backside as near to the water's edge as she dared and stretched her tail towards him. 'We're so glad to see you, we've been so scared!' she sobbed as he grabbed her scales.

At last the Dragon Master was next to them, stroking their necks. 'So, what's been going on? I've been looking for you three scallywags since sunset,' he said quietly.

All three of them started talking at once: 'Sparky was telling Maurice... And Clarys was pretending... Then Maurice fell in the mud...'

'It's all my fault,' admitted Clarys at last. 'I just can't help teasing Maurice.'

'But it was my idea...' moaned Sparky.

'And I fell for the stupid trick because I get worried about my looks,' groaned Maurice.

'And we're all very sorry and we're so glad to see you!' added Clarys, nuzzling him with her nose.

The Dragon Master scratched their ears. 'And I'm very glad I found you. It's too dangerous to move from here tonight, so I'll stay with you until Ember and Flamethrower come for us in the morning. The tide has turned and the sky is getting lighter, so they won't be long now.' Then the Dragon Master spread his cloak over their backs and organised their tails so they didn't get wet. And at long last, the little dragons stopped shivering.

When dawn warmed the skies with red and silver,

six dark dragon shapes appeared in the south. Everyone shouted, waving wings and tails until the dragon flight wheeled in, scooped up each of the miscreants in their claws, and headed for home.

It took hours of swimming in the sea and being rubbed down with Pumice's special soapweeds to get the mucky dragons clean. Even the Dragon Master had to have a bath, but he insisted on having a rock pool heated for him. He said he'd had enough of cold water for a very long time.

When all four had eaten breakfast by a roaring fire in Pumice's cave, the Dragon Master peered under his bushy eyebrows at Maurice, Clarys and Sparky.

They wriggled uncomfortably, waiting for the BIG telling off.

There was a long silence, then he said, 'That was a very dangerous prank.'

'Sorry,' they squeaked miserably.

'Hummm. I should think so too.' Then he smiled. 'Now go out and play, but be kinder to each other in future.'

'Aren't you going to send us to our caves for a

whole week?' Maurice asked timidly.

'I think you've all learned your lessons. Just don't be so silly again, any of you! Go on! *Shoo!*' the Dragon Master laughed, clapping his hands.

With just the merest glance in a rock pool to see if his scales were tidy, Maurice led the others out of the cave and into the welcoming sunshine.

One by one, they stretched their sparkling wings and lifted gracefully up into the sky.

Flying the West Wind

One autumn day, Pumice wanted to tidy her cave but she ached all over. At last, she crawled onto her nest and closed her eyes. She just wanted to sleep.

That evening, when Treasure returned home with a small shark that Igneous had caught, she found Pumice shivering. Treasure lit a fire and tried to coax Pumice to eat, then piling dried seaweed over her friend, she curled up next to her to sleep.

In the morning, Pumice didn't speak or move.

Her dragonfire was out.

Distraught, Treasure ran through wind and rain looking for the Dragon Master. But all the caves were empty and everyone was out fishing.

Frightened and exhausted, Treasure went home at last, but her cave was chilly, dark and very still.

Treasure sat down next to Pumice and cried. She felt so lost and alone.

She didn't hear the Dragon Master step quietly into the cave. She only felt his warm hand stroking her head gently.

Sniffing loudly, she hugged him and sobbed.

'I heard you calling,' he said. 'I came as soon as I could.'

Together, they knelt next to Pumice. She was very cold. 'Look, her dragonfire has gone out,' Treasure said softly, touching her friend's nostrils. 'Light it again for her Dragon Master. She needs her warmth. She's so old and tired.'

The Dragon Master wiped away a tear and in a choking sort of a voice he whispered, 'Indeed, little one, her dragonfire has gone out. It will never burn again. She is dead.'

Treasure gripped his hand in her claws. 'Couldn't the West Wind make her alive?' she begged. '*Please!*'

The Dragon Master smiled a little and hugged his Treasure. 'Then she'd feel ill and old again. It is time for her aches and pains to be over.'

'But won't she ache worse without dragonfire?'

The Dragon Master kissed Treasure's nose. 'No, for now she's with the West Wind and flying as she has never flown before. We'll talk about it later, but right now I can hear the other dragons returning. They'll want to weep with you. Crying is good. Pour your grief out.'

Then the Dragon Master unfolded a big hankie, leaned against the noble dragoness and sobbed.

Pumice's funeral was sad and beautiful. Her body had been taken to lie on the seashore. The dragons decorated her with shells and ribbons of seaweed in twisting patterns up and down her grey-blue sides. They gathered around her in the Great Circle and sang songs of the winds and sea. Then each dragon took turns to talk about kind things Pumice had done or to share a special memory.

When they had finished, there was silence.

'It's you now.' Flamethrower gently nudged Treasure forwards.

Too scared to speak and her throat aching with crying, Treasure simply hugged her friend. Dear old Pumice who had loved her and looked after her when some of the others had said she'd be useless. 'Thank you,' she whispered in the old dragon's ear. 'I don't think I ever told you I love you, I hope you knew.'

Then she kissed the kind, tired face. 'I don't want you to hurt or to ache any more. Goodbye. Fly well.'

With that, the Dragon Master said very softly, 'Now we shall give her back to the fire and wind that gave her birth.'

And the dragons raised their wings and breathed glowing flames that caressed and warmed the old dragon's bones for the last time.

When the funeral was over, Flamethrower took Treasure back to his cave and offered her supper but she couldn't eat. Silently, she lay down near the fire and closed her stinging eyes.

When the night was quite dark, something woke her.

It was the Dragon Master whispering, 'Treasure, come with me. We must go flying together.'

Thinking she was dreaming, Treasure followed him down to the beach where the West Wind was playing all around them. Harder and harder it blew, until the friends were swept off their feet. Treasure squealed, but the Dragon Master hugged her. 'Don't be afraid. The West Wind has something to show us.'

Before Treasure could ask what he meant, the Wind roared even more loudly, tossing them up into the night. On, on, it chased, cradled and buffeted the travellers, rolling and spinning them high amongst trillions of piercing, icy stars.

Treasure, who usually hated flying, felt no fear.

At last, the darkness softened and gave way to a different sort of dawn with a light that felt... *alive*! And there Treasure floated, bathed in the kindly brightness. Quiet. Safe. No pain. No grief.

And the light filled her with tingling excitement and energy.

Treasure leaped up, laughing like a hatchling dizzy with her first flight. Filled with joy, she could go anywhere, do anything. She was *in* the Wind and it was in her! She didn't understand how, and she didn't care.

Then just as suddenly, her dancing stopped.

There was Pumice.

She was flying with magnificent silver wings that arched triumphantly above her head as her shimmering green-blue body snaked through the air.

This was the *real* Pumice, no longer grey and crumpled with pain.

Treasure gasped and felt herself falling.

Sweeping close, Pumice laughed and nudged

Treasure aloft. 'Fly, little one, don't be afraid!'

And Treasure flew in the laughing Wind.

Treasure did not remember returning to her cave, but the Dragon Master took her home and tucked her up safely.

When she woke, she ate a good breakfast and went for a swim. As she rolled in the waves, wondering if her flight had been a dream, she saw the Dragon Master waving at her. She splashed ashore to meet him.

They walked awhile, then they sat on a cliff top and looked out across Kilve bay.

'I'm glad you took me with you last night,' Treasure said. 'I'm very sad that Pumice is dead, I've still got lots of crying to do, but now I've flown with the West Wind, I understand. There's nothing to be frightened of, is there?'

'No, little one. All is well.' Then the Dragon Master put his arm around her. 'I'm glad you came. I feel better now, too.'

Then the friends squeezed hand and claw and sat silently watching the waves for a very long time.

How Pumice
Lost Her Wings

After Pumice died, everyone felt very sad. No one felt like playing or fishing.

About a week later, the Dragon Master spread out his cloak so the little dragons could cuddle up to him. The older dragons lay close by, sunning themselves on the rocks. The Dragon Master's cloak was very special. If he pulled it over them at night, the stars came out and exciting dreams filled the dragons' heads. When he spread it on the ground they were about to hear tales that would make their spikes tingle with delight.

The Dragon Master smiled at his friends as he stroked their blue-green scales. 'You are about to hear a very important story,' he said. 'A true one. And today, Treasure will do the telling.'

Treasure sat right in the middle of the Dragon Master's cloak with her tail curled and head held high. When everyone was still, she began, her voice squeaking a little with nerves. 'Pumice forbade the telling of this tale while she was alive. It's the story of how she lost her wings.

'Long years ago, when the world was made from earth, water, wind and fire, many strange creatures were born. Each one was given a special friend, a Master or a Mistress to look after them.

'The terrible serpent Leviathan has her Mistress, as do the wild unicorns, and the Behemoth has his Master. As you know, the Behemoth's task is to guard fiery secrets deep under the earth. There, in the ever-seething ocean of molten lava, he is king.

'One day, the monster looked out of a volcano crater and saw our green fields and forests. The Behemoth was jealous. He wanted to own all this too, so he decided to pour fire over the world and make it his home.

'The Behemoth Master thought this was a good idea. He liked power and he wanted to use the secrets of the earth and sea to rule over the unicorns, Leviathan – and even us dragons!

'So between them, they decided to make war. In those days, Flamethrower was only a hatchling and Fizzle's hearing was so sharp he could hear a worm wriggle a mile away.'

'That must have been a long time ago!' muttered Sparky.

Ember poked the young dragon with a claw. 'Be quiet!'

Ignoring them, Treasure continued. 'In those days Pumice was a cross little dragon who was only good at eating fish and moaning. Nothing was ever right, or good enough for her. She was only really happy when people were admiring her beautiful silver wings.

'It was nothing to her that the Behemoth was on the march. Nor did she care about the evil magic woven by his treacherous Master, who was misusing the deep secrets entrusted to him. The monster and his Master belched fire, ripped up rocks and crashed continents into one another. Wherever they went, the face of the earth was scorched and ruined.

'One day, word came that the battle was raging towards our land.

'All the dragons, even the little ones, flew to turn the Behemoth back. They had to protect Midnight Forest with all its animals!

'Only one dragon didn't go to the battle. That was

fussy little Pumice, who refused to do anything to help. She was cross because the others weren't at home looking after her. She didn't see any point in chasing the Behemoth. That was the Dragon Master's job!

'Day after day, she sat sulking by the sea, wishing the noise of battle would go away and that someone would come back.

'One rainy night, when Pumice was all alone at home, five sopping wet goblins trouped in to her cave. Without noticing Pumice was curled up in the shadows at the back, they lit a fire.

'These woodland creatures usually live under fallen tree trunks and down little holes, so Pumice couldn't make out why they had come to Kilve. She had a feeling they weren't friendly, so she stayed very quiet and still, listening to what they were saying.

'"I don't understand where the dragons can be," said one.

'"The Master will kill us if we don't find them," replied another.

'"No, he won't," said a third, "He'll pull our wings and legs off, one by one, just as he promised."

'The others fell silent and shivered at the thought of such a terrible fate.

'Pumice shrank back, well out of sight. She felt cold

and afraid. She was certain they weren't talking about the *Dragon* Master. He would never do anything like that.

'"Well, where are the dragons?" repeated the first goblin. "We have to find them quickly. They're all that stand in the way of the Behemoth's total victory tomorrow."

'The first goblin beckoned his fellows closer. "Our orders are to keep the dragons busy here, so our army can burn the Midnight Forest and destroy the Dragon Master. Then the whole world will be a burning desert and the Behemoth will be king."

'"But I like our forest," protested a young goblin.

'"I don't remember the Dragon Master being dreadful," piped up another. "I remember him being kind... understanding."

'"Bah! Kindness is weakness!" scoffed a third voice. "The Behemoth and his Master know," and here he whispered... "*wonderful* secrets!"

'"What sort of secrets?" gasped the others.

'"Secrets from the depths of the earth. Secrets from before time began – special secrets the wishy-washy Dragon Master is too scared to use!"

'"Tell us! Tell us!" begged the others.

'"No!" he snapped. "These things are forbidden to all but the powerful! Now. Let us find food and more wood. The dragons must be hunting. They'll return soon and we must be ready for them." And they left the cave.

'Pumice sat rigidly still for a few minutes, then she made up her mind. She must find the Dragon Master and warn him.

'The war had come to her. She had to act.

'At the back of Pumice's home there was a narrow crevice which opened into an underground passage some way inland. She had often explored it when she was very tiny. It was tight then. She knew she had little chance of getting through it now she was older and bigger but she had to try. Short of fighting the woodland goblins (and their teeth looked very sharp) the crack was her only escape.

'Luckily, Pumice had eaten so little while she'd been sulking, she'd become very thin. Folding her wings tightly she managed to wriggle her way along and out to a windy hillside, well out of sight of Kilve and the goblins. It was early morning and still raining. She didn't have the faintest idea how to find the Dragon Master. She hadn't seen anyone for days. She had never felt so alone.

'She tried to roar and breathe fire to make herself brave, but tears trickled down her nose and put the flames out, leaving nasty-tasting smoke in her mouth.

So, taking a deep breath, Pumice spread her wings and flew into the sky, wheeling left and right until she saw smoke rising over the farthest reaches of the Midnight Forest.

'She set her course that way. Grey clouds were piling inland on a stiff breeze. She thought, *If I hide in the clouds, I might find the others without being seen.* She'd never flown that high before, but up she soared and hovered just inside the grey mist.

'Soon she could see the cause of the smoke. The dragons were there, locked in a terrible fire-battle with all sorts of strange creatures that she had never seen before – friends of the Behemoth from the deepest earth! But the cloud she was hiding in was scudding beyond the battle.

'*Should I break cover and try to reach my friends?* Pumice wondered.

'But the West Wind whispered, "*Keep going!*" So on and on she flew. The clouds around her became thicker and blacker, until she could hardly see. A stench of burning and sulphur filled the air and Pumice could hardly fly for coughing.

'At last, she heard a shout. It was a voice she knew! Could it be the Dragon Master?

'"Coming!" she tried to call, but the words stuck in her throat as the smoke burned her lungs.

'Down she plummeted. She couldn't breathe for fumes. She couldn't see through the darkness. All around echoes rumbled, was she inside something?

'Then came another shout. She speeded her steep spiral down until a fire glowed. Heat scorched her belly and wings.

'She was flying into the heart of a volcano! Flames rippled over her as she plunged. She called again.

'Then came a reply! She squinted in the burning light; a dark shape was huddled on a ledge. The Dragon Master!

'And wading through the molten lava towards him was the heaving bulk of the Behemoth. On the monster's shoulder stood his evil Master, swathed in a blood-red cloak with his arms raised. He pointed a short staff at the Dragon Master and chanted words that crashed like rocks.

'The Dragon Master wrapped his cloak of stars tightly around him. His wild hair was shining red from the glowing fires. He was trapped and afraid, but above the volcano's roar and the beast's howling, Treasure heard him shout, "I don't want your secrets! They are poison!"

'The Behemoth Master laughed. "If you don't work with me, I will kill you, then all your precious dragons will be in my power. It's a simple choice!"

'Through the smoke and gloom, Pumice saw the Dragon Master look up, as if searching for a chink of real light amid the searing fireglow. "Come West Wind and blow," he called clearly.

'Pumice didn't hesitate. Swiftly she swooped down, and with one flick of her wing she knocked the Behemoth Master backwards. He fell for a long time, a black spinning dot against the boiling white heat.

Then he was gone.

'The Behemoth stared stupidly. He didn't seem to understand what was happening. Without his Master, he was only a great lumbering beast.

'Pumice hovered next to the Dragon Master, who scrambled onto her back. As soon as his arms were around her neck, she leapt up, climbing towards the sky that she knew was somewhere above.

'Her wings and belly burned. She couldn't breathe and was losing height. The Dragon Master was too heavy for her.

'"Help!" she whispered into the stinking dark.

'Suddenly, there came a mighty roar from below as the Behemoth realised he'd been robbed of both his Master and his prey by a scrawny dragoness.

'He belched flames and smoke, catching Pumice in its full force.

'But the blast tossed them upwards and out into the

open air! With the last fragments of her wings, Pumice glided to a safe landing on cool, green grass.'

Treasure stopped and swallowed hard, then she burst into tears, so the Dragon Master took up the tale.

'We were found by the Mistress of the Unicorns,' he began. 'Her magical creatures have the power to heal with one touch of their horns. With the help of this lady and her beasts, I recovered quickly, but what was left of Pumice's wings had to be cut off and the unicorns healed the stumps. Then they ran to find the other dragons, so we could be carried back to Kilve.'

There was a long silence.

At last Maurice whistled. 'Wow! Fancy Pumice defeating the Behemoth Master! We never realised she was so special.'

The Dragon Master smiled and rubbed Maurice's scales in that nice scratchy place between his wings. 'She was no different from you. Pumice was just a sulky little dragon who wouldn't clean her cave. When the time came, she saw something she had to do and she did it.'

'I could never do anything like that!' Clarys shook

her head sadly.

'You never know what you can or can't do until the time comes.' The Dragon Master said kindly.

Then he stood up and shook out his cloak, spilling little dragons everywhere. 'And talking of time,' he announced, 'the sun is setting. I must light the stars and all good dragons must go to bed.'

So that is just what they did.

The Day
the Nidhogg Came

Winter passed and the days grew long again. The fishing was good and the skies were warm. The dragons grew fat and contented. No one argued, no one played nasty, muddy tricks on anyone else, and Sparky hadn't asked 'why?' for a whole week.

'I wish it was like this all the time,' sighed Horace.

'Someone's bound to spoil it!' grumbled Maurice.

'It's bound to be Clarys,' said Horace.

'Why?' asked Sparky innocently.

Clarys was wondering whose tail to twist first, Horace's for being rude, or Sparky's for saying 'why?'

when the Dragon Master came puffing and panting up the slope.

He sat on the grass and spread his wonderful cloak so the little dragons could curl up next to him. He usually did this when he was about to tell a story, so everyone was pleased.

But this time there was no story. He looked serious. 'I fear the Nidhogg is coming,' he said sadly. The older dragons glanced nervously at each other.

'You mean he's *real*?' asked Ember. 'I thought he was just in stories.'

'He's very real,' The Dragon Master went on. 'He's an earth monster. He isn't big, in fact he can be difficult to spot, but when he does turn up it's very bad news.'

'What does he do?' gasped the little dragons.

'He nibbles away at the roots of everything we love,' the Dragon Master sighed. 'He turns good things inside-out and upside-down. He brings chaos.'

'Like my cave?' chirped Sparky.

The others promptly sat on him to make him shut up, but the Dragon Master smiled. '*Much* worse than that! Now, you'll have to look after each other when he comes. And always remember what you *know* to be true.'

The day the Nidhogg came was still. Not just calm, but eerie. The skies were silent for all the birds had flown, the fish had swum away and the forest animals had slipped between the trees.

And worst of all, no one knew where the Dragon Master was.

Standing on his hind legs, Flamethrower flapped his wings and roared, 'Make the Great Circle everyone. *Now!*'

As they gathered on the beach, a thundering noise filled the air. A huge wave was rumbling ashore, swept by a howling wind. Closer and closer the wave came, until the sky seemed filled with water and the sea-bed was empty.

The terrified dragons flew to higher land. Ember scooped up Treasure just as the swirling water crashed and foamed around them, cracking rocks and lashing the cliffs.

Everything was upside down and inside out!

Wet and terrified, the dragons clung onto each other. They held their breath and no one moved...

Then Clarys snapped at Sparky for treading on her tail. Horace stepped out of Clarys's way and knocked

Maurice downhill by accident. Maurice scrambled back up and thumped Horace. Fawkes and Fireworks argued about who should stand where. Through it all, Fizzle kept munching his chocolate biscuits, until Sparky told him very slowly and clearly that he was a deaf old fool. Fizzle cuffed Sparky around the ear, making him cry. Treasure said he was a stupid little baby and Igneous and Furnace threatened to set the place alight if everyone didn't stop arguing.

'Stop it! STOP IT!' roared Flamethrower, spitting orange fire. 'What would the Dragon Master say?'

Everyone stopped shouting. Embarrassed, they shuffled from foot to foot. Clarys said it was Horace's fault. Furnace said it was Sparky. Igneous said it was Maurice and he'd never liked any of them anyway, and Treasure began to cry.

Then as suddenly as it started, the strange storm stopped.

In the silence that followed, a sneering, giggly voice called out, 'Hello. I'm Nidhogg. I've come to play with you.'

The dragons looked around, then drew back, for in the grass by their feet was a grey slug-like creature. And it was laughing!

'Stamp on it!' yelled Furnace, but they all rushed to the same spot so fast their heads cracked together!

Staggering back they glared and snarled at each other.

'There he is!' Maurice called out. 'The slug-thing's crawled up that tree and it's sneering at us!'

As the its mouth to laugh, green goo dripped out.

And it seemed a lot bigger than it had been.

Again, the dragons rushed at it, only to collide with the tree, tangling their wings and bumping their heads once more.

'Stand back!' ordered Igneous, belching a huge ball of fire. This only reduced the tree to ashes and scorched Flamethrower's wings.

Flamethrower dived at Igneous with bared teeth and claws. If he hadn't tripped over Clarys' tail on their way, he'd have done terrible things to the young dragon.

'STOP!' yelled Treasure. 'Can't you see what's happening? *We've* been turned inside out too. Nidhogg has got between us!'

'Nonsense!' scoffed Igneous. 'I've just fried him!'

'No, she's right,' said Flamethrower. 'Look!'

And there, on the grass, were thick slime trails weaving in and out, up and down and all around, even over their beautiful scales!

'Ugh!' said Maurice. And he wiped at the muck with bundles of grass but only succeeded in spreading the gloopy mess further.

And right in front of them sat the fat, slobbering Nidhogg.

The dragons were about to launch at him again, when Treasure piped up: 'Don't! Can't you see? He gets fatter on us arguing. The more we all rush to kill him, the more we get in an angry tangle and that makes everything worse! It's not each other we have to fight, it's *him*!'

Flamethrower nodded. 'Right! Igneous, you and I have the strongest dragonfire. Together we will burn this thing to cinders!'

The other dragons drew back. There was silence, except for a silly giggling noise from the creature.

Flamethrower and Igneous breathed deeply, flapped their wings and blasted their dragonfire as hard as they could!

But the Nidhogg slipped away, and instead of scorching flames, only water poured from the dragons' nostrils.

The others laughed.

Igneous and Flamethrower swung around, flashed their claws and lashed their tails. 'Silence everyone!' roared Flamethrower. 'We must concentrate on the Nidhogg.'

Then Horace spoke up. 'I could grab it, fly away and drop it a long way out to sea.'

Everyone agreed that would be an excellent idea.

Horace crept up on the Nidhogg. It was getting bigger and laughing more loudly every minute. Horace crept closer, snatched the thing in his claws and sprung towards the clouds. But the harder he flew, the more he found he was getting nowhere. Horace struggled, flapped and wheeled but he hardly rose above the hillside.

The Nidhogg breathed in and Horace was sucked backwards. Thump! He landed in a crumpled heap, upside down and covered in sticky slime.

Gleefully, the Nidhogg wriggled out from the dragon's claws, cackling loudly.

The dragons were getting very frightened. They couldn't think what to do, and what was worse, the Nidhogg was swelling bigger every second. It would soon be longer than Sparky.

Treasure called them all into a huddle. 'We've tried all our weapons,' she said, 'but we haven't thought about what *he* uses.'

'*Slime*!' groaned Maurice.

'And nasty laughter,' added Clarys.

'What can we do against that?' asked Flamethrower.

'We could put wax in our ears,' suggested Furnace.

'That's a good idea,' said Treasure, 'but we'll have

to finish our council of war first.'

'I wish the Dragon Master were here,' moaned Clarys.

'Well, he's not!' Flamethrower said firmly. 'So we've just got to do our best and not let it matter.'

'You're right!' said Treasure. 'Now, the Nidhogg's favourite weapon is to turn things inside out. When he's around, we argue. He makes tiny accidents feel like terrible crimes.'

'And he turned the sky into the sea, and the sea into the sky!' added Maurice.

Then Horace, who was still shaky from his adventure added, 'My flying became a horrid sucking-dropping-y-ness.'

'So,' said Treasure, 'if the Nidhogg turns everything inside out, we've got to make things right again.'

'How do we do that?' asked Fireworks.

'Perhaps I could ask him why he's doing it?' suggested Sparky doubtfully.

Treasure patted his back. 'That's a great idea. Try, it might give us a clue.'

Sparky felt scared. 'Dare I?' he asked.

'You're the only one who can,' Treasure smiled.

Slowly, Sparky walked to where the Nidhogg was gloating in the grass. It seemed a bit smaller now. That was comforting. It was still giggling, but in a worried way with its mouth wide open. Sparky noticed it hadn't cleaned its teeth. What a grimy little monster!

Sparky took a step forward.

The Nidhogg wriggled back.

Sparky took another step forward.

The Nidhogg squiggled even further back.

Sparky looked down at the creature, first out of one eye, then out of the other. 'Excuse me, sir,' he added doubtfully. 'Why are you doing this?'

The Nidhogg looked up and sneered. 'Because you all think you're so big and important with your posh scales and fancy wings. But you're nothing. *Nothing*!'

'But that's not true!' said Sparky, beginning to cry. 'That's not right at all!'

'But you're all *stupid*. You're *nothing*, the lot of you!' it squeaked, shrinking rapidly.

'Everyone does stupid things sometimes,' Flamethrower added carefully, 'but the Dragon Master loves us just as we are, so we can't be nothing.'

As he spoke, the creature became smaller and smaller.

One by one, the other dragons piped up with, 'And we love each other really, even when we tease,'

'That's true!'

'Hear, hear!'

And the Nidhogg kept shrivelling until it was no bigger than an old balloon. It wriggled away and with a scrabbling of stones it slid over the cliff.

With the smallest of splashes, it was gone.

A few minutes later, the Dragon Master arrived, his cloak flapping in the wind behind him.

'Oh, Dragon Master!' the dragons shouted, tumbling down the slope towards him. 'We do wish you'd been here, we've had such a terrible time!'

'Of course I was here,' said the Dragon Master gently. 'But if you'd been able to see me, you'd have expected me to fight for you, like baby dragons. You had to learn to tackle the Nidhogg for yourselves.

'And you did well. You learned that squashing, dropping and blasting him just didn't work. Whatever you did turned upside down and inside out. The crosser you became, the bigger the Nidhogg grew.'

Treasure nodded. 'When we stopped arguing, he lost his oomph!'

'Then I asked the Nidhogg *why* he was doing it!' laughed Sparky, jumping up and down.

Everyone clapped their wings.

'So all your "whys" have been useful at last,' smiled Flamethrower, 'And I am very proud of you for being so brave.'

Sparky grinned.

'Then,' added Maurice, 'when we found the Nidhogg wanted to make us feel grey and slimy like him, the answer was easy,'

'We just had to think about the truth, just like you said.' And Treasure gave him a big hug. 'We remembered how much you love us and how much we love each other, then everything turned right side out again. The Nidhogg couldn't argue with that because it was all true – even if we forget sometimes.'

Horace roared in delight, sending flames into the sky. 'It worked. He shrivelled up and wriggled away!'

'Hooray!' roared the others, blasting their dragonfire too.

And they made such a noise the Dragon Master had to cover his ears.

Treasure Hunt

The Dragon Master had a secret. No one knew what it was, but they guessed something very important was about to happen for he had asked everyone to get ready for a very big party.

For days on end, the dragons had stacked driftwood for a huge bonfire on a flat rock above the high tide mark.

Fireworks mixed his special powders for a magnificent coloured smoke display. Maurice and Sparky planned an aerobatic fly-past and, as a special treat, Flamethrower and Ember had promised to sing!

It was all very exciting. Everyone was so busy catching small sharks and making oyster sauce and seaweed bread, no one stopped to wonder why such a magnificent feast was happening. It wasn't even the Dragon Master's birthday.

The evening of the party came at last. Everyone drank, ate, flew, danced and sang, until dawn began to show above the inland hills. Tired and happy dragons gathered quietly around the fire's dying embers.

Then the Dragon Master stood up. 'We've had a lovely party.'

'Hear! Hear!' boomed the bigger dragons.

'Cool!' squeaked the littlest ones.

The Dragon Master smiled sadly. 'And now, the time has come for me to say goodbye.'

There was a long, shocked silence.

'Not forever,' he added gently, 'but I will be away for about a year. I must go to the land of fire and ice because my cousin, the Mistress of the Eastern Dragons, has asked for my help. It will be a long journey, but I won't forget you for a single moment.'

'But how will we manage without you?' asked Ember in horror.

The Dragon Master smiled and opened his arms wide. 'Everything you will ever need is right here.'

'What if the Nidhogg comes back?'

'What is there to be frightened of? You've defeated

him once. You all know what you have to do.'

A few of the smaller dragons began to cry and the Dragon Master hugged them all, one by one. 'I'll return as soon as I can, and the Unicorn Mistress has promised to graze her beasts on the fields nearby. In very great need she'll send her white stallion to gallop the clouds to find me.

'Now,' he said, springing to his feet and tossing his cloak back over his shoulders, 'I've a game for us to play before I leave at nightfall.'

The dragons didn't feel like playing, but they listened.

The Dragon Master spread his arms. 'Hidden here at Kilve, there are three great treasures. They are very valuable indeed. I want you to find them and bring them here, then you'll see you have everything you need to look after yourselves until I return.

'Now, get some sleep. Return at high tide then the game will begin.'

The weary dragons dragged themselves back to their caves. Everyone felt so unhappy after all the fun of the party. A few scattered to lonely places and slept where they were. Others sifted through their hoards, looking for their most prized possessions.

But what sort of 'treasure' did the Dragon Master want?

At high tide, they all met around a roaring bonfire, but the dancing light and comforting heat did nothing to cheer the unhappy dragons.

'Well?' asked the Dragon Master, 'what ideas have you had?'

The older dragons called out, 'Cave brooms!' and 'Fish drying racks!'

'Real treasure has to be beautiful,' protested Maurice.

'Like pearls and corals?' offered Clarys, who had plenty of both.

The Dragon Master just smiled. 'Maybe, but I'll give you a clue: you might not be able to *see* the very best treasures.'

Immediately a hubbub broke out, but the Dragon Master would say nothing more, and he went away to pack.

Tempers were fraying badly, and the Dragon Master hadn't even left!

At last, in desperation, Treasure asked Flamethrower to make everyone be quiet and take their places for the Great Circle. Tired, curious, and grumpy, the dragons arranged themselves around Treasure who climbed onto Fizzle's back so she could be seen.

'What do you think the Dragon Master means by

"valuable treasure"?' she asked, gazing at the sad blue-green faces.

'Beautiful! Useful! Strong! *Edible!*' yelled fifty different roars and squeaks.

Treasure held up a claw and everyone fell silent. 'Let us think,' she said. 'If the Dragon Master is going away for a while, what will be the most valuable things we can have?'

There was a long silence, then, 'Good weather.'

'Plenty of fish!'

'Nothing nasty around...'

'Definitely no sluggy-things!' came the replies. Then the arguments started again.

Fawkes flapped his wings noisily. 'Those sorts of things don't count!' he sneered. 'Anyway, as the treasures are invisible the game's not fair.'

Furnace growled at Fawkes. 'The Dragon Master only said we *might* not be able to see what we're looking for, so good weather and no slug-creatures *could* count.'

'Same thing,' sneered Fawkes and he went into a sulk.

Igneous was about to 'accidentally' breathe some rather hot air onto Fawkes's tail, when Treasure called for silence again. 'Let's all go away, calm down and think,' she urged. 'It's probably all very simple and right under our noses. The Dragon Master would never ask us to do the impossible!'

One by one the dragons drifted away.

Fizzle went to his cave and looked long and hard at his chocolate biscuit hoard. He knew everyone would laugh if he presented *that*. But what else could he offer? He'd go and have a chat with Fireworks.

At that moment, Fireworks was poking a claw into various bottles, smiling as he imagined bangs, stinks and gloriously coloured smoke rings. Gleefully he took down his very best jar of powder. It was sky-blue-pink-with-purple-spots. When that was put into rockets, the display would be glorious. It'd bring happiness to everyone.

But that was only one treasure. He'd go and ask Fizzle what he thought.

Maurice took down his pot of scale polish. How could life go on without that? The second treasure had to be floating in warm air on a summer evening, but the third baffled him. He would ask Clarys.

Meanwhile, Clarys was deep under the hills with her collection of pretty pebbles. Carefully she chose a clear white stone that turned sunlight into brilliant colours. She loved it best of all, but she didn't mind sharing. Hidden in the cave it was only a piece of rock. Out in the sunlight, it would glisten and make the others feel happier. She looked about for a second and third treasure, but she couldn't decide.

She would go and ask Sparky.

Sparky was floating somewhere above the clouds. Since he had learned the answer to 'why?' he'd became really good at flying and fishing. Diving out of the sky into the sea was perfect joy to him. He'd bring a few salmon to share at the meeting and tell the others about catching them.

Might that count as *two* treasures? He'd ask Horace.

Horace looked up and smiled at the sun. *That* was what he loved best. He filled a bucket of water, staggered with it to the meeting place and put it where it caught the brilliant golden light. Sitting next to the bucket, Horace remembered how the others had flown to catch the real sun for him.

'They cared about me!' He smiled. 'If it wasn't such a sad day, I'd be ever-so happy.'

Igneous and Furnace lay on a hilltop and puffed little golden tongues of flame into the clear blue afternoon sky. How they loved fire! What blazes they had made! What rock falls they had caused when they'd cleared the streams in the Midnight Forest! Surely fire was the greatest gift any dragon had. But the second and third treasures baffled them.

'It's got to be roast shark with samphire and seaweed sauce!' Igneous announced.

'No,' Furnace replied firmly. 'It was the day we found Treasure.'

'You're right, but what about number three? Let's go and see Treasure now,' Igneous replied. 'She'll know the best answer.'

Far in the distance they saw Treasure walking along the beach, poking at various bits of seaweed, tasting this and scratching that. Even though she was young she knew a great deal about plants.

Treasure sighed and tried not to cry. It was getting late and the Dragon Master would be going soon.

Further up the beach, Fireworks was piling wood onto the bonfire. The others were gathering around him with all sorts of bundles in their claws: glittery things, wriggly things, bulky things, bags of things and tiny, secretly hidden things.

All of them treasures.

By early evening, the tide was high and the clear green water surged and fell, wreathing the rocks with foam. Still and forlorn, the dragons were seated around their best friend.

The Dragon Master stood up. His cloak sparkled in the setting sun. 'Well, my wise friends let me see what you have brought.'

One by one all the dragons laid their precious things on a flat rock in the centre of the circle. But before they sat down again, they each whispered something into the Dragon Master's ear.

Treasure watched the pile grow. Everything was so different. She was worried. There were bound to be arguments about whose gift was the best. Then there'd be sulking because this and that hadn't been chosen. She wasn't looking forward to calming everyone down.

When her name was called at last, Treasure crawled forward and presented the Dragon Master with a small pile of lava weed. 'It saved our lives,' she began quietly. 'We were caught by a storm and stranded in the middle of the sea for days. This was nearly all we had to eat.'

She looked sad. 'But that's all I've brought. I couldn't possibly decide what else to suggest until I've heard what the others think.'

Then there was silence.

The Dragon Master stroked his beard as he surveyed the pile of precious things. No one could guess what he was thinking.

What was treasure and what was rubbish?

At last the Dragon Master threw back his head and laughed. Then he took off his cloak and threw it into the air. One by one, the twinkling stars came out and shone on the dragons' scales and wings until they shimmered with dancing light.

Then the Dragon Master exclaimed, 'You've done better than I hoped! You've each told me the same thing – you all wanted to talk to the others before choosing. This is your first treasure: wanting to work things out together.

'Next, here we have everything from diamonds to chocolate biscuits. It'd be impossible for you all to agree on your second precious thing, because you see different things as important. Your "differentness" is your second treasure: being yourselves.

'Lastly, no one has laughed or teased, or called anything rubbish. That is your third treasure: loving and respecting each other.

'Now you have found the three great secrets you had hidden here, I am certain you can look after yourselves. Care for these things well and I will be back sooner than you think.

The Dragon Master's voice choked. 'May you fly with the West Wind while I am gone.'

118

Treasure pushed her nose into her friend's hand. 'You don't want to go, do you?' she asked softly.

The Dragon Master wiped his eyes and sniffed. 'No, I'd much rather be here, but I must help my cousin. More importantly, you need me to go away.'

Treasure's eyes widened in horror. 'No we don't...'

The Dragon Master shook his head. 'When you were young, every time something was difficult, I sorted things out for you. And that was right.

'Now, you are older. If I don't go away sometimes, you won't learn to fly the West Wind for yourselves. Today you have found a new kind of wings. You are growing up fast and other creatures will learn from you.

'Tonight I must go. Tomorrow, there'll be new adventures for all of us.'

The Dragon Master gave his beloved dragons sleep. Taking one last, loving look at his silver-winged creatures, he stepped into the shadowy edges of the Midnight Forest where a white figure was waiting.

Wrapping his cloak around his shoulders, the Dragon Master mounted the huge unicorn and rode away into the dark.

Note from DCHQ:

Many kind readers of this book have contacted me at **DCHQ** with concerns that the **Dragon Eggs** at **Kilve** are **Shockingly Treated** and even **Neglected.**

Rest assured, **All Is Well.**

DRACONUS KILVUS lay their eggs near the water's edge to be **Washed Away** by the next **High Tide. Salt Water Toughens the Eggshell, protecting** a baby dragon as it grows (a process of 2-300 years). On land once more, **Rain Softens the Shell** and makes **Hatching** easier.

Such is the magic of **Kilve** that almost all dragon eggs are found just at the right time.

Signed

Agent Green

Draconics Expert & Chief Liaison Officer
Dragon Conservation Head Quarters
Cotswolds, England

To find out more about **Beth Webb**
and her magical children's stories, go to:
www.bethwebb.co.uk
or click on:
www.marchhamilton.com

See more of cover artist **John Ralls'** painting on:
www.studioelix.com

Dragon Conservation HQ
Can be contacted on
www.midnightstorytellers.co.uk/wb/pages/dragon.php